The Masterpiece Adventures   BOOK THREE

TROUBLE at SCHOOL

for MARVIN & JAMES

ELISE BROACH

Illustrated by
KELLY MURPHY

SQUARE
FISH

Christy Ottaviano Books

Henry Holt and Company • NEW YORK

SQUARE
FISH

An imprint of Macmillan Publishing Group, LLC
175 Fifth Avenue, New York, NY 10010
mackids.com

Our books may be purchased in bulk for promotional, educational, or business use. Please
contact your local bookseller or the Macmillan Corporate and Premium Sales Department
at (800) 221-7945 ext. 5442 or by e-mail at MacmillanSpecialMarkets@macmillan.com.

Library of Congress Cataloging-in-Publication Data
Names: Broach, Elise, author. I Murphy, Kelly, 1977– illustrator.
Title: Trouble at school for Marvin & James / Elise Broach ; illustrated by Kelly Murphy.
New York : Henry Holt and Company, 2017. I Series: The masterpiece adventures ;
book 3 I Summary: Marvin the beetle finds adventure when his
human friend James takes him to school.
Identifiers: LCCN 2016016207 (print) I LCCN 2016052446 (ebook)
ISBN 978-1-250-18338-5 (paperback)   ISBN 978-1-62779-319-3 (ebook)
Subjects: I CYAC: Beetles—Fiction. I Human-animal relationships—Fiction.
Friendship—Fiction. I Schools—Fiction. I BISAC: JUVENILE FICTION / Readers / Chapter
Books. I JUVENILE FICTION / Animals / Insects, Spiders, etc. I JUVENILE FICTION /
Social Issues / Friendship.
Classification: LCC PZ7.B78083 Tr 2017 (print) I LCC PZ7.B78083 (ebook) I DDC [Fic]—dc23
LC record available at https://lccn.loc.gov/2016016207

Originally published in the United States by
Christy Ottaviano Books/Henry Holt and Company
First Square Fish edition, 2018
Book designed by Anna Booth
Square Fish logo designed by Filomena Tuosto
The artist used pen and ink on Coventry Rag paper to create the illustrations for this book.

3   5   7   9   10   8   6   4

AR: 3.4 / LEXILE: 620L

For my friend Laura Forte, who's always
up for some fun or trouble
—E. B.

To the best schoolmates:
Karen, Michael, and Anne-Marie
—K. M.

Contents

CHAPTER ONE

Marvin Goes to School

It's early morning, and Marvin is watching James get ready for school.

"I have Art today," James says. "Mr. Chang is the best. I wish you could meet him."

Marvin has heard James talk about the art teacher before. Mr. Chang tells James, "There are no mistakes, just happy accidents."

This means that if you do something wrong when you're making a picture, it isn't really wrong, because it leads the way to something new.

Marvin tries to remember this when he makes pictures of his own.

For instance, when he's drawing a flower and his leg slips, he can turn the flower into a rabbit, like this:

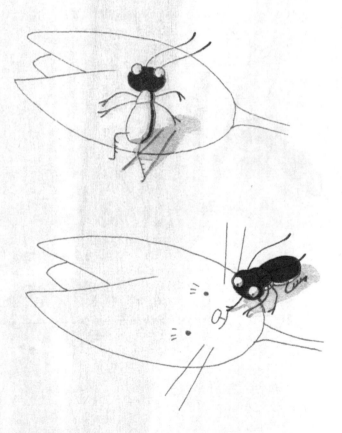

Or when he's drawing a starfish and he makes too many points, he can turn it into a dinosaur, like this:

"Hey," James says suddenly. "Why don't you come to school with me?"

Marvin can't believe what he is hearing.

School!

He has always wanted to go to school with James. He's so happy that he runs around in circles.

James laughs. "Does that mean yes? We have to hurry! You can ride in my pocket."

James puts his finger on the desk. For one second, Marvin thinks of Mama and Papa. He knows he should ask them about going to school with James. He thinks they probably wouldn't like it.

But there isn't time. And anyway, he is so excited! He's going to *school*! At school, James has a whole life that Marvin knows nothing about. Now he will get to see James's friends. He will go to Art class. He will hear what Mr. Chang has to say about happy accidents. It will be amazing!

Marvin runs toward James's finger and takes a flying leap.

James lifts him up and drops him gently into his shirt pocket, where Marvin can peek out. Then James grabs his backpack and yells, "Bye, Mom!"

"Good-bye, dear," says Mrs. Pompaday. "Don't forget your lunch." She hands him the brown padded lunch bag that keeps his food cool.

"Ba ba, ya ya!" says William, who is in his high chair, eating breakfast.

And then James swings open the front door of the apartment, and they are on their way to school.

First, they go down the hall.

Then they ride in the elevator.

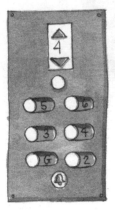

Then they are out on the street.

Marvin loves going outside with James. It's a pretty fall morning. The air is crisp and the leaves are turning red and orange and gold. Marvin is snug inside the warm pocket as he peeks over the top.

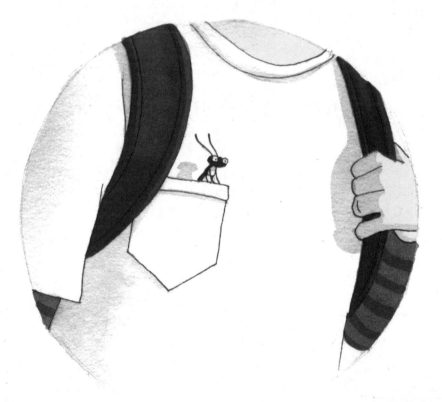

The city is full of new sights and
sounds. Marvin sees a lady walking five
dogs on leashes. He hears the loud, long
honk of a taxi horn. On a street corner,
a man is playing a violin.

James walks for several blocks, in the shadows of tall buildings. People rush past. Cars rush past. Leaves flutter onto the sidewalk.

"Here we are," James tells Marvin finally.

They climb the steps to a big building.

This must be school!

The first thing Marvin notices about school is that it's very noisy. The second thing he notices is that it's very crowded. There are kids everywhere! They are pushing and hurrying through the halls, laughing and talking with their friends.

"I have to go to my locker to drop off my backpack," James whispers to Marvin.

Soon they are standing in front of a wall of metal lockers, and now some kids are talking to James.

"Hi, James!"

"James! Over here!"

Marvin is glad that James has friends at school. Marvin knows he is James's best friend so he wants what's best for James . . . and having human friends is good for James.

"Art is first," James tells Marvin.

Yay! Marvin will finally meet
Mr. Chang.

The art room has colorful pictures all
over the walls. There are big tables in the
middle of the room, and at each table are
pencils, paints, crayons, and markers.

So many art supplies! Marvin can't
wait to get started.

Mr. Chang has spiky hair and it is
blue. Marvin has never seen blue hair!
He wishes beetles had hair so his could
be blue.

"Hello, class," Mr. Chang says. "Today we are working with pastels. Come choose a picture of something you'd like to draw." He holds up a box. Marvin can see that it is full of postcards. There are postcards of places, flowers, animals, and cars.

monarch

James reaches into the box and pulls
out a postcard of something . . . a bright
orange butterfly!

A butterfly isn't as good as a beetle,
but it's close. James sits at a table by
himself. He sticks his finger in his pocket.
"Do you want to help?" he whispers to
Marvin.

Of course Marvin wants to help! It has been so long since he's had a chance to make a picture with James.

Mr. Chang says, "Think about color. Think about touch. Look at what's on your postcard and draw what it would *feel* like if you touched it."

Marvin has seen butterflies in the park with James. He thinks about how a butterfly might feel, so light and free.

He watches James draw the butterfly. James waits a minute, to make sure nobody is looking, then sets Marvin down on the edge of his paper.

He puts an orange pastel crayon
near Marvin and crumbles a little of
it in a pile.

Marvin crawls across the paper
to the orange pastel. Gently, he rubs
his feet in the orange dust and begins
to draw.

CHAPTER TWO

Lunch

Marvin draws and draws. While James draws the outside of the butterfly, Marvin colors the inside. He uses his legs to make tiny, swishy orange lines all over James's butterfly.

"Wow!" James says. "That's great."

"What did you say, James?" Mr. Chang asks.

"Nothing," James says quickly, but it is too late.

Mr. Chang is coming to their table. *Uh-oh!* As fast as he can, Marvin runs over to the pastels and crawls on top of the black one. He tries to blend in enough that Mr. Chang won't see him.

But Mr. Chang isn't looking at the pastels. He's looking at James's picture.

"James," he says. "This is amazing. I love what you've done with the butterfly's wings. Now, what about drawing some thicker black lines over the orange, to show the pattern?"

Marvin can't draw thick lines, but James can. James picks up the black pastel and hides Marvin with his hand. "Okay," he tells Mr. Chang. He draws thick black lines while Marvin holds tight to the crayon.

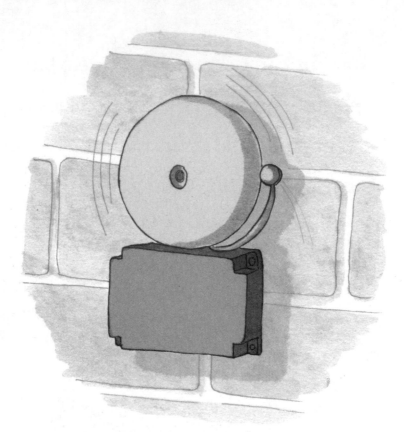

"Good work," Mr. Chang says. He walks back to the front of the room.

In a little while a bell rings, making a loud

brrringgggggg!

"That means Art is over," James whispers, putting Marvin back in his pocket. When Marvin looks down at the paper, he sees that he and James have made a beautiful butterfly. Together!

The rest of the morning goes quickly. James has Math, then Spanish, then Social Studies. Marvin likes Social Studies best.

There is a globe in the Social Studies classroom, just like James's globe at home. The classroom globe is on the bookshelf next to James's desk. When nobody is watching, James puts Marvin on it. Marvin crawls all the way from Africa to the North Pole. When James spins the globe, Marvin feels dizzy. He has to sit down on the desk and rest.

Then the bell rings and it's lunchtime.

"Are you hungry?" James asks Marvin. "Let's see what my mom packed for lunch."

With Marvin still in his pocket, James gets his lunch bag and goes to the cafeteria.

Marvin quickly figures out that he does not like Lunch. The cafeteria is very noisy. People are everywhere. Big brown trays bang on the tables. Marvin is afraid to leave James's pocket.

"It's okay," James whispers to him.
"I'm going to put you in my lunch bag.
Nobody will see you, and you can eat
whatever you want."

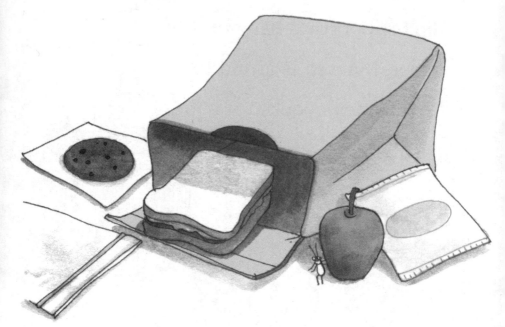

James unwraps all his food. There is a
sandwich, a bag of potato chips, an apple,
and a cookie. He hides Marvin behind
the apple.

"Hey, James," calls one of James's friends. "I'll trade you my banana for your potato chips."

"No, thanks," says James. "I like my chips." Marvin is glad because he also likes chips. James crunches a potato chip in his hand so that the crumbs fall next to the apple. Marvin sneaks out and grabs a tiny piece of potato chip, then hides again.

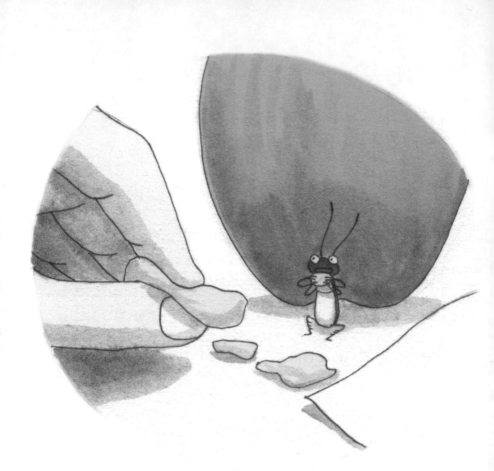

The potato chip tastes salty and good.
James tears off a tiny bit of his turkey
sandwich for Marvin. It's yummy.

James starts talking to his friends.
Marvin begins to feel safer. He decides
to climb on top of the apple to have a
look around. He will be quick about it
so nobody spots him.

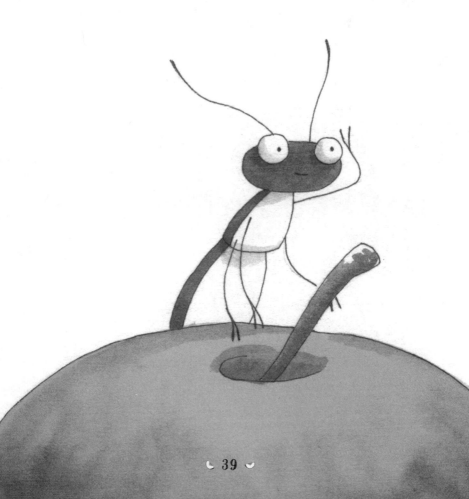

Carefully, he crawls over the round, hard skin of the apple. It is so smooth that he falls off at first. But finally he's near the top. He can see the whole cafeteria, big and sunny and full of kids.

Suddenly, that loud bell rings again:

brrringgggggg!

James starts to close up his lunch bag. Marvin is about to climb down from the apple when one of James's friends leans forward, and . . .

Ahhh-CHOO!

He sneezes!

The sneeze sweeps Marvin into the air. He is turning over and over in the wind, when he lands on a cafeteria tray.

Bip!

Ow! It hurts. He is on his back, waving all of his legs, trying to turn over. He's so afraid someone will see him!

All at once, he feels the tray moving.

Oh no.

He can see the round face of a boy
above him, but at least the boy doesn't
see him. The tray bumps and sways,
and Marvin slides back and forth on
his shell.

Then, with no warning, the tray turns over! Marvin falls, tumbling through the air in a litter of food and wrappers and empty cartons.

He lands in a big, dark, smelly place.

Where is he?

And where is James?

CHAPTER THREE

Buried

At first, Marvin is too surprised to be scared. He is no longer on his back, so that part is good. But as soon as he tries to crawl through the mess of stuff, more stuff falls on top of him.

Food and trash are raining down on Marvin, banging him on the head, bouncing off his shell. He crawls inside a white plastic yogurt container to protect himself. All around him are pieces of sandwiches, half-eaten crackers, fruit, napkins, milk cartons, juice boxes, and candy wrappers.

Marvin has never seen so much food. Or so much trash! He is buried.

It's dark in this place. How will James ever find him?

After a while, the rain of food stops.

The voices fade.

It's quiet.

Where did everyone go? Marvin must try to get out of here.

He crawls out of the yogurt container. What is this place?

There is trash in every direction.
Marvin decides it must be a trash can,
even though it is much bigger, darker,
and smellier than the Pompadays'
wastebaskets in the apartment.

Marvin sighs. If he were with his parents, or even his cousin Elaine, he might want to eat some of the yummy food that is all around him. Why, there's a chocolate cookie right next to him! And Marvin loves chocolate. But it's not much fun to eat tasty things by yourself. And besides, he is too worried.

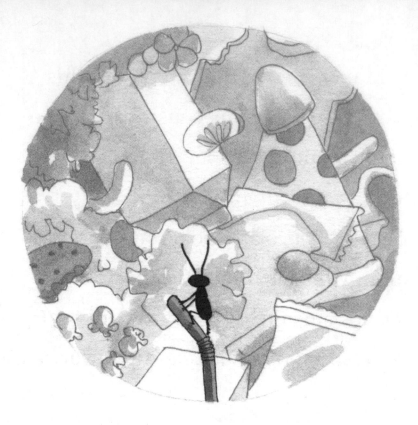

How will he get back to James? James probably didn't even see what happened to him. Maybe James thinks he crawled back into the lunch bag. And if James doesn't know where he is, how will Marvin ever get back home to Mama and Papa?

Just thinking about Mama and Papa,
who don't know that Marvin is at school,
makes him want to cry.

"Hey, why so sad, little fella?"

Marvin freezes. Who is talking
to him in this dark, scary place?
Then he sees who it is:
a cockroach.

Marvin knows about cockroaches. There used to be cockroaches at the Pompadays' apartment, until the terrible, unforgettable day when the exterminator set roach traps. An exterminator is a human who kills bugs.

This cockroach is long and skinny and brown. Marvin stares at him.

"Can't you talk?" the cockroach asks.

Marvin tries to be polite. "Yes," he says. "I'm lost."

"What do you mean, lost?" the cockroach asks. He crawls over to Marvin.

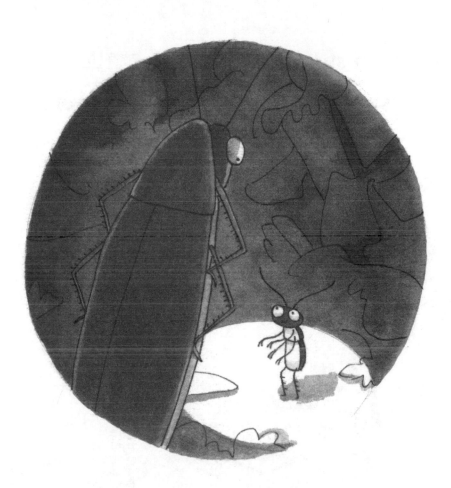

Marvin is a little afraid. And anyway, how can he explain? He can't tell another bug that his human friend brought him to school. "I'm not supposed to be here. I fell in," he says.

"Not supposed to be here?" the cockroach exclaims. "Look around you, boy! This is heaven. Have you ever seen so much food in your life?"

"I'm not very hungry," Marvin says, backing away from the cockroach.

The cockroach snorts. "Of course you are! Help yourself, little fella. Cookies, cake, cheese, grapes . . . whatever you want, it's yours."

"I just want to get out of here," Marvin says.

The cockroach shakes his head. "You
young ones are so spoiled these days.
You don't know how to be thankful for
what you have."

"It's not that," Marvin tries to explain. "I just want to go home."

Suddenly, he feels hopeless. There is so much trash. He has no idea how far it is to the top of the can.

The cockroach seems to realize how
upset Marvin is, because he says quickly,
"Okay, okay, don't cry. I'll help you."

"Really?" Marvin asks.

"Sure. I don't know where your home is, but I can take you up to the top. Follow me." He climbs onto a banana peel, waiting for Marvin.

Marvin crawls through the darkness over the wet, sticky peel.

"This way," the cockroach tells him, climbing over a crust of bread.

They keep going, up and up and up. They crawl over an apple core, a candy wrapper, and a carton of milk. They crawl over brown paper bags and half-eaten slices of pizza.

They climb and climb, through the jungle of trash. Marvin follows the cockroach over an orange peel and onto a cracker box that is squashed flat. After a long while, Marvin can see tiny slivers of light high above him.

His shell is wet and covered with crumbs. He smells terrible. They keep climbing. Now the light is streaming down on them.

"Keep going, little fella," the cockroach says. "We're almost there." He crawls over a juice box. Then he climbs up a thin, bent straw.

Marvin grabs the straw with both of his front legs and inches up it. They are almost at the top now.

"Here you go," the cockroach says. "But I have no idea why you'd want to leave a feast like this. You can still get out once they tie the bag shut, you know."

Marvin doesn't even want to think about that. He climbs out on top of the pile of garbage. Finally!

He can see the white tile ceiling of the cafeteria, the bright lights, and the black rim of the trash can surrounding him.

"Oh, thank you!" Marvin says to the cockroach. "Thank you for helping me."

"No problem," says the cockroach. "Good luck!" He waves, then disappears back into the pile of garbage.

Marvin is alone again. The cafeteria is empty and quiet. It feels like a long time since lunch. How will he find James? And if he can't find James, how will he ever get home?

CHAPTER FOUR

See and Be Seen

Marvin doesn't know what to do. Now that he's at the top of the trash can, he can climb out. But he will have to crawl all the way down to the floor. And once he does that, where will he go?

He thinks of the busy halls of the school. They go on forever, with so many pounding feet. And he doesn't know which classroom belongs to James.

He is wondering what to do when he sees a sparkling red Life Saver candy stuck to a napkin.

Mama loves Life Savers. It's her favorite kind of candy. Just thinking of Mama makes Marvin long to be home.

He crawls over to the candy and takes a tiny bite. The sweet cherry taste perks him up.

Brrrrinnnnng!

The bell rings loudly in the empty room. Is James going to another class now? Has he forgotten Marvin? Marvin hears a lot of noise in the hallway outside, and the sound of many feet.

Then he hears voices coming closer, into the cafeteria.

"Well, that's it," says a man.

"I'll get the bags in the kitchen, you get the ones out here," says another man.

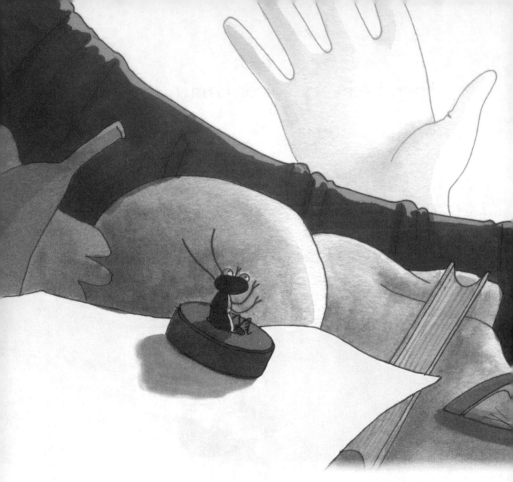

Marvin hears footsteps coming close
to his trash can. A man's big face looms
over him. Marvin ducks inside the red
Life Saver, trying to hide. The man's
hands grab the big bag that holds all
the trash.

By the time Marvin realizes what's
happening, it is too late.

This man is emptying the trash! He's
going to pull the trash bag out of the
can—with Marvin inside—and dump
it somewhere!

Marvin is frantic. He has to get out of the bag before the man ties it shut. He races as fast as he can over the bumpy surface of food and litter.

"Hey! Wait a minute!" A boy's voice cuts through the air.

Marvin would know that voice anywhere.

JAMES!

James is here! James is looking for him.

"Excuse me, Mr. Winter," says James, "but I think I dropped something in the trash by mistake. Can I look before you take it away?"

Mr. Winter stops what he's doing. "You'll never find it in here, kid. We'd have to dump out the whole thing."

"Please," James says. "Can I look?"

"What was it?"

"It was a . . ." James stops. "A toy," he says finally.

"What kind of toy? What does it look like?"

Now James's face is over the trash
can too. Marvin's heart leaps with joy.
But how can he get James's attention?
If he moves, Mr. Winter will see him.

And there is so much trash! He needs to go somewhere he will be seen. If he crawls onto something white, maybe James will notice his shiny black shell.

Marvin sees the white napkin under the Life Saver. He tucks the red Life Saver under one leg and waves his front legs in the air.

For a minute, he doesn't think James saw him. But then, suddenly, the napkin closes over Marvin and rises up through the air.

"I found it!" James says quickly.

"You're kidding," Mr. Winter says. "Right on top?"

"Yes, it was right on top. In the napkin." James's voice is full of relief.

"Well, that was lucky for you. A
minute later and everything in this bag
would be outside in the Dumpster."

Marvin can't bear to think about
that. Through the white wall of the
napkin, Marvin hears Mr. Winter tying
the bag shut and banging the trash can
back down onto the floor.

"Thanks, Mr. Winter," James tells him. "Sorry to bother you."

Marvin is still inside the napkin. Then it is very loud, and he can tell they are in the hallway.

"Are you okay?" James asks softly, opening up the napkin. "I thought I'd lost you!"

Marvin clings to his cherry Life Saver. He is shaking from fear and relief.

James's eyes are huge. "I was so scared! I kept coming back to the cafeteria between classes, but I couldn't find you anywhere."

Marvin beams with happiness. The whole time he was looking for James, James was looking for him! Because that is what friends do.

"Good thing you had that red Life Saver," James says. "That was the first thing I saw, when you made it move. It really *was* a lifesaver." He smiles down at Marvin. "I'm going to put you back in my pocket, where you'll be safe. School's over now. We're going home."

Gently, he takes Marvin out of the napkin and drops him into his shirt pocket.

Marvin is still holding tight to the cherry Life Saver. What an adventure he's had! He cannot wait to be back in his little home under the Pompadays' kitchen sink, with Mama and Papa, Uncle Albert and Aunt Edith, and even Elaine.

CHAPTER FIVE

Happy Accidents

When James finally sets Marvin down inside the kitchen cupboard and closes the door, Mama and Papa come rushing out to meet him.

"Marvin!" Mama cries. "Where were you?"

"You were gone all day. What happened?" Papa asks.

"I was with James," Marvin answers slowly. "At school."

"AT SCHOOL!" Mama and Papa shout together. They are not happy.

"Marvin, what were you thinking?"
Mama says. "That is way too dangerous!"

"And you didn't tell us," Papa adds.
"You must always ask before you do
something like that."

"I know," Marvin says. "There wasn't time."

"If you don't have time to ask, you don't go," Mama tells him. "That's the rule."

"I'm really sorry," Marvin says. He knows Mama is right. Then he remembers what he has for her. "Mama, I brought you something!"

"A cherry Life Saver!" Mama smiles. "We'll have it for dessert tonight."

Papa is pleased too. "That's Mama's favorite. Where did you find it?"

"At school," Marvin says. He thinks about the trash can, but decides not to talk about that just yet. He follows Mama and Papa through the little hole in the wall into the beetles' home.

Mama takes the Life Saver and puts it in the center of the pink eraser that is their dining-room table.

"Ewww," Mama says. "Darling, you smell terrible."

"I know," Marvin agrees.

"School must be a very smelly place," Papa says.

"It is," Marvin tells him.

"Well, you need a bath."

Mama and Papa take the juice bottle cap that is Marvin's bathtub, and together they push it under the leaking hot-water pipe beneath the kitchen sink. As it fills with water, Mama drops tiny bits of soap into it, to make bubbles.

Marvin slides into the warm, soapy water. He swims around, kicking his legs. He loves to swim.

Elaine comes over. "Marvin! Where were you?" she cries. "I thought you'd been stepped on. Or eaten by a mouse! Or zipped into a pocket where we would never see you again."

Marvin thinks she seems very excited by all these terrible ideas.

"I'm fine," he says. "I went to school! With James."

"School!" Elaine says. "Oh my goodness. What was it like?"

And she leans over the side of the
bottle cap while Marvin tells her all
about school.

He tells her about Art class and
drawing the butterfly. He tells her
about spinning on the globe. He tells
her about the sneeze during lunch that
blew him away from James. He even
tells her about meeting the cockroach.
He swims through the warm water,
telling her about everything he saw
and did.

"Oh, Marvin," Elaine says, "you must never, ever do that again."

Marvin knows she's right. But even though it was scary, he's still glad he got to go to school.

He saw things he had never seen before.

And that's when Marvin knows
that it's not just mistakes in *art*
that are happy accidents.

Mistakes in life can be happy
accidents too.

Because even if a mistake is
scary, it can help you see something
differently.

And it can lead you someplace new.

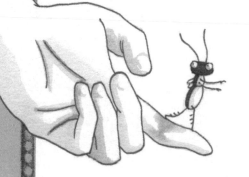